The First Day of School

Robin Hill School

Written by Margaret McNamara
Illustrated by Mike Gordon

Ready-to-Read
Aladdin Paperbacks
New York London Toronto Sydney

For Becky & Chester and Michael & Cookie
—M. M.

❦
ALADDIN PAPERBACKS
An imprint of Simon & Schuster Children's Publishing Division
1230 Avenue of the Americas, New York, NY 10020
Text copyright © 2005 by Simon & Schuster
Illustrations copyright © 2005 by Mike Gordon
All rights reserved, including the right of reproduction in whole or in part in any form.
ALADDIN PAPERBACKS, READY-TO-READ,
and colophon are registered trademarks of Simon & Schuster, Inc.
Also available in an Aladdin library edition.
Designed by Sammy Yuen Jr.
The text of this book was set in Century School Book.
Manufactured in the United States of America
First Aladdin Paperbacks edition July 2005
2 4 6 8 10 9 7 5 3 1
Library of Congress Cataloging-in-Publication Data
McNamara, Margaret.
First day of school / Margaret McNamara ; illustrated by Mike Gordon—1st Aladdin
Paperbacks ed.
p. cm—(Ready-to-read) (Robin Hill School)
Summary: After a summer of playing with his puppy, Michael is sad to learn that she
cannot stay with him on the first day of school.
ISBN 0-689-86914-2 (pbk.)—ISBN 0-689-86915-0 (lib. bdg.)
[1. First day of school—Fiction. 2. Schools—Fiction. 3. Dogs—Fiction.]
I. Gordon, Mike, ill. II. Title. III. Series.
PZ7.M232518Fg 2005 [E]—dc22 2004016672

Michael loved his puppy.

Her name was Cookie.

All summer long,

Michael played with Cookie.

They played catch.

They played ball.

They were always together.

On the night before
the first day of school,
Michael said to Cookie,

"Tomorrow we start
first grade."

In the morning,
Michael walked to
Robin Hill School.

His mom and Cookie
came with him.

When they got to school,
Michael said to Cookie,
"Time to go to school!"

"Oh, Michael," said his mom,
"dogs are not allowed
in school."

"What?" said Michael.
"Nobody told me!"
He hugged Cookie tightly.

Mrs. Connor was the
first-grade teacher.
She saw how sad
Michael was.

"May I pet your dog?"
she asked.

"I guess," said Michael.

"He looks nice,"
said Mrs. Connor.

"She is a she,"
said Michael.
"Her name is Cookie."

"I wish Cookie
could come
to school,"
he said.

"Me too," said Mrs. Connor.
"You do?" asked Michael.

"Oh, yes,"
said Mrs. Connor.
"If Cookie came to school,
she could live
on the playground.

She could sleep
in a cubby.

She would belong
to everyone
at Robin Hill School!"

Michael gave that
some thought.
"Mom," said Michael,
"you can take Cookie
home now."

Michael had a good
first day.

But he missed Cookie.

When the day was over,
Cookie was waiting for him.

She waited for him
every day,
because she was his dog.